I0720191

HALF HIGH

ALSO BY RICHARD BRUCE NUGENT:

Gentleman Jigger

HALF HIGH

RICHARD BRUCE NUGENT

WITH AN INTRODUCTION BY
WHIT FRAZIER

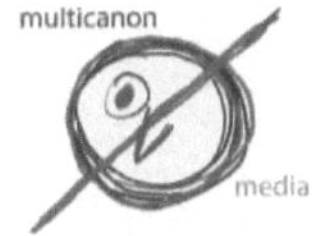

The Multicanon Media Company, LLC
New York

First Edition
Published in the United States by
The Multicanon Media Company, LLC

www.multicanon.com

Paperback ISBN: 978-1-7372149-6-0
ebook ISBN: 978-1-7372149-7-7

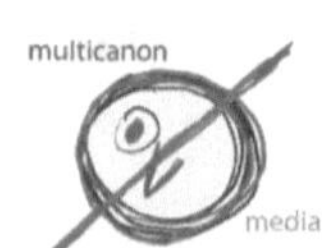

The Multicanon Media Company, LLC
45 Rockefeller Plaza, Suite 2000, New York, N.Y. 10111

for

CECCO

because he thinks the sun is an orange
And the moon is a persimmon.

HALF HIGH

RICHARD BRUCE NUGENT

TABLE OF CONTENTS

INTRODUCTION

This is an unusual introduction, in that it functions as something like an introduction not only to this book, but also as an introduction to Multicanon Media Company itself. This unorthodox approach to introducing a new publishing company, not to mention to introducing a new book, is fitting because Multicanon's mission is one which is itself highly unusual, and which warrants a little explanation. The general mission of Multicanon Media is to publish Black authors whose work has gone unrecognized and has fallen into the public domain. This mission is just a launching point for the company; ideally I would like to expand the publishing venture into not only multimedia (hence the name) projects, but also to publishing writers whose work is overlooked by traditional media companies. To some extent, I have already begun doing this, and the website already features a multimedia page where I have current multimedia projects posted that are freely accessible.

As I am new to publishing however, and am learning on the job, I want to begin with a project which aligns with my general interest in canon studies – which is to say that I am interested in broadening the canon to include authors and works who ought to be in the canon but have been overlooked. Although Multicanon Media is a tiny venture, and one that is not bound to attract much attention, I do hope to make works that are not readily available more available to researchers who are interested in obtaining them, as well as to readers who might delight in them; I also hope that by placing works that researchers are looking for alongside works that they may not be looking for, I will increase the critical appraisal of Black authors who have not received the amount of critical attention they deserve. Ultimately, I hope to introduce Black texts to the world that might have otherwise gone unnoticed. After all, as a Black writer myself, I am the beneficiary of the work and struggle those living-departed have already done. This venture is my small contribution towards honoring their legacy.

All of which is to say that the start of Multicanon Media began, unbeknownst to me at the time, on Friday, March 19, 2010. On this day the Leon Levy Center for Biography in Midtown Manhattan held a one-day symposium on "The End of Biography." The keynote speaker was Arnold Rampersad, the official biographer of Langston Hughes, whose two-volume opus I had just finished reading. I was, at the time, deep into research for my own first novel, *Harlem Mosaics* (also published by Multicanon Media), so hearing Rampersad speak was of great interest to me. More than that, I hoped to have the opportunity to maybe speak with him briefly. I was luckier in this regard than I expected. Not only was Rampersad there, but so were David Levering Lewis, whose *When Harlem Was in Vogue*, is the cornerstone go-to text for studying the Harlem Renaissance, as well as the late Hazel Rowley, who wrote an important biography of Richard Wright; and finally, and most importantly for this project, the late Thomas H. Wirth.

Tom, as I would come to call him over our brief correspondence, was close with Bruce Nugent, and had become his literary executor after Nugent's passing. Shortly before the start of the conference, I spoke briefly with Dr. Rowley, and told her about my project. She gave me, in turn, some great tips on ways that I could improve my research results, and after Dr. Rampersad's keynote speech, she was kind enough to introduce me to Rampersad, Levering Lewis and

Tom Wirth. This is to say that without her help, I would never have been in the position to publish this book in the first place.

In any case, Tom and I discussed *Gentleman Jigger*, Nugent's only (until now) published novel, which I was halfway through at the time. Tom gave me his card and told me to write him once I had finished reading the book. A week later I sent him the following long email (although all emails printed here are edited for brevity):

Dear Mr. Wirth,

I met you last Friday at the Leon Levy Center for Biography. At the time I was exactly halfway through Bruce Nugent's *Gentleman Jigger*, and you asked me to write you once I finished it. Well, I've finished it now (actually just a few hours ago), and so now I'm writing as promised. My ideas on it are still only half-formed, so I hope you have the patience to read through my still stumbling thoughts while I try to arrange them... It really is something of a mess of a novel... though I wonder how interested Nugent would have been in writing something less messy... It seems like he wants *Jigger* to be an exploration of his character and relationships, and how those relationships affect his character as he matures through early adulthood; and Bruce is a complex character: a pastiche of different interests, passions and ideas... It took me a while to learn to read it this way... I guess the natural thing to do, especially with Part One is to compare it to *Infants of the Spring*, - and as much as I like Wallace Thurman, Thurman really is more of a journalistic than novelistic writer (at least in *Infants*) - and maybe the reason for that is simply the difficulty of writing imaginative fiction about real events. Bruce does the same thing more successfully, and I think it's because he's enough of an egoist to revel in the idiosyncrasies of his character. With Thurman, we seem mostly to get a crippling neuroses.

I should say *Infants* had a huge effect on me. I must have read it in three days, and while at the time, I couldn't help notice things about it that irked me as a reader, (the long, often stilted discussions, the flatness of the prose), I also found it completely compelling. I don't think I've had that kind of relationship with a book before - where it annoyed and engrossed me so much at the same time. I also connected with Thurman the author; his concerns about art and race, art and how one lives one's life, insecurities about his work and the need for other artistic foils; these were things I related to in a really immediate way. It started to change the way I thought about literature, in general: how it functions, who it's for, why it's worth living for, and the strange, almost Vampiric relationship it has with a writer's life.

Alain Locke and Charles S. Johnson in particular, as thinkers, also influenced me. The faith they had that a real arts movement could form out of so mishmash and unlikely a crew of artists as we find in the Harlem Renaissance - and the fact that it was successful (and I think it was successful, with reservations), sort of made me rethink a lot of the ways I approached literature. It goes along, I think, with something Rampersad said during his speech last Friday: how he spent so much time studying and critiquing literature, that finally he wanted to get away from all that; it seemed to be the wrong way to approach something that you love. [...]

Sincerely,

Whit Frazier

Tom responded back right away with the following:

Dear Whit,

I can't thank you enough for your extended and thoughtful commentary. As one who was not trained in literary criticism and who is reluctant to be judgemental, I find your impressions both interesting and valuable.

I also have difficulty reading JIGGER as a novel rather than a memoir. Bruce stated on more than one occasion that everything in INFANTS (and therefore the Harlem part of JIGGER) was literally true except for the death of Paul Arbian. Bruce said Wallie killed him off because he had to end the novel somehow. Whether the death of Thurman himself so soon after the publication of INFANTS was purely happenstance, or whether Thurman projected his own suicidal thoughts onto Arbian is an interesting question.

I can send you the key to most of the characters in INFANTS and JIGGER if you'd like.

Aeon is indeed problematic. You're surely correct that he is loosly based on Toomer. I think there's a missing section dealing with his death in more detail. I had to put JIGGER together from several manuscript fragments, none of which was complete. There were complete chapters, but their sequence had to be inferred from internal evidence to make the flow logical. It's quite possible that some things were missing entirely.

Bruce later wrote a shorter companion piece called HALF HIGH. It narrates the story from Aeon's point of view (in a style that parodies Gertrude Stein). My first thought was to shuffle the chapters of HALF HIGH and JIGGER together. My editor convinced me that that would interrupt JIGGER's narrative flow (as well as create problems of length). I didn't resist his suggestion that HALF HIGH be omitted, because I was reluctant to exercise so much editorial license to begin with. But it would have made Aeon's death much clearer.

If you'd like, I can email you the manuscript of HALF HIGH (which is complete and in proper order, unlike so many of Bruce's other manuscripts).

Anyway, thanks again for your thoughts.

Best, Tom

Unfortunately, Tom never did send me the key to who's-who in the novels, but he did send me *Half High*, which is, of course, the work presented here. To my mind, *Half High* is a much more solid work than *Gentleman Jigger*. This should come as no surprise as *Half High* was, as Tom mentioned, complete, whereas *Gentleman Jigger* needed to be assembled from fragments, and thus, as a text lacks the coherence that is present here. Moreover, *Half High* does the important working of making clear the bridge between the downtown younger modernists and the Harlem Renaissance modernists. This connection is already clear in a text like Jean Toomer's *Cane*, but *Half High*, by taking elements from Gertrude Stein (which I read as pastiche instead of parody), Arthur Schnitzler, Jean Toomer himself and the bohemian counterculture tradition in literature, gives us one of the clearest expressions of Black modernism from the Harlem Renaissance that we have.

Half High **As Black Modernism**

Nugent's novella, *Half High*, can in fact be read as a discussion of the relationship between Black and white modernism, with Nugent suggesting that through the combination of the two, something like a new form – echoing Toomer's concept of a new race – comes into being. Toomer's concept of a new race is best portrayed in his long poem "The Blue Meridian," which was first published in *The New Caravan*, a 1936 anthology of Black poets. Toomer's idea in this poem, largely derived from his own mixed heritage, was that the American was a new race – a blue race – which would usher in the next age of mankind. This idea was near and dear to Toomer's heart because not only did Toomer have enough of a mixed background as to appear nearly white in some photographs, but he also had a proud Black lineage to his name as well, with his maternal grandfather being Pinckney Benton Stewart Pinchback, who had the distinction of being the first Black governor in America. Pinchback was himself of mixed heritage, and according to W.E.B. Du Bois in *Black Reconstruction*, he looked more like Andrew Carnegie than Frederick Douglas. Nonetheless, Pinchback chose to embrace his Black heritage and used it to help the plight of Black people in post-Reconstruction America. This example surely would have been inspiring to the young Jean Toomer, whose book *Cane* is an exploration of the African American past and African American folklife, folklore and tradition as seen in the south, in the mid-Atlantic and in the north.

Thus, in *Half High*, Aeon's character, who is obviously influenced by Jean Toomer, becomes something of a literary device in Nugent's hands to explore this concept of the *blue modernist*, or the new race of human that comes about as a result of being an American and a modernist. The color blue is also noteworthy, as this seems to have echoes in the blues tradition which poets like Langston Hughes were so interested in exploring in poetry. This blue modernist, in the character of Aeon, is the modern American, who is both Black and white and yet neither; who is both attacked by whites for being Black and attacked by Black people for being white; who is, ultimately, something of a religious figure in that he will be necessary to bring America beyond its racialized insanity. That the novella takes the form of a biographical novel, where the reader follows Aeon from his childhood to his death makes sense when read as the life of a quasi-religious figure who is meant to signal the arrival of a new type of human. To this end, Nugent's narrative follows the structure of many narratives of persecuted spiritual leaders, and this structure is meant to inform the way we read the text.

Also of interest is the fact that the story is told in a series of relationships. As with *Gentleman Jigger*, which uses some of the same characters as *Half High*, the characters in this story are generally stand-ins for real people. For example, while it has already been established that Aeon, the main character of *Half High*, is Jean Toomer, other characters can also be identified with real people. Stuartt, the ultimate bohemian, is Bruce Nugent himself, which is clear when one reads this book alongside *Gentleman Jigger*; Tom Wirth was convinced, after extensive research, that Myra was Dorothy Peterson, a discovery which he wrote to me excitedly about upon his realizing it; and finally, I read the character of Siempre as Georgia O'Keeffe, as the references to Taos, the fact that she is a painter, and the storminess of her relationship to Jean Toomer seem to fit the character. Unfortunately, I only came up with this idea after Tom passed, so I was not able to run the theory by him, but the more I read this text, the more I am convinced that Siempre is indeed meant to be O'Keeffe, and this just solidifies the connection between the Black and white modernist sensibilities displayed here.

Another thing Nugent was able to do writing this novel from the perspective of Jean Toomer was to re-write the passing novel completely. Nella Larsen had already done something like this with her short novel *Passing*. She completely reimagined and rewrote the so-called tragic mulatto character in the novella, turning this tragic figure into something like a heroic character, whose death is not one of pathos, even if it is nonetheless mired in the mystery of the question of what we can know. Indeed, everything is murky in Larsen's *Passing*: questions of sexuality, fidelity and infidelity, race and class, and even ultimately how Clare dies are all brought into scrutiny, and there is never a good answer at hand; we actually can't know anything, Larsen seems to be telling us, and what passes for knowledge is only knowledge within the context of a worldview that conforms with how we already understand things; taken from a different perspective or worldview, what might be true from one angle might be false from another (for a fascinating discussion of this, see Gabrielle McIntire's article, "Toward a Narratology of Passing: Epistemology, Race, and Misrecognition in Nella Larsen's *Passing*).

Half High picks up where *Passing* leaves off, and gives the reader Harlem as presented through the eyes of Jean Toomer, or Aeon, a character who moves almost too fluidly between the Black and white worlds. He passes when he does not want to pass, visits brothels in Black neighborhoods and is accused of being a white man engaged in racialized sexual tourism. Aeon's Du Boisian double consciousness gives us a Harlem that could never be the Harlem of the ultra-dark Wallace Thurman, for whom the idea of passing was not even a remote possibility; nor is it the Harlem of Bruce Nugent, who could, and does go downtown and pass for Spanish in *Gentleman Jigger*, but is still always Black in Harlem. No, in *Half High*, Aeon is almost forced into being neither Black nor white, as neither group can fully accept him as one of their own; there is no home to Harlem for Aeon. Whereas the reader has seen Aeon already in *Gentleman Jigger*, Aeon's cross-racial relationships are foregrounded in a way in *Half High* that they aren't in the previous novel. Perhaps more importantly, because Nugent is writing about Toomer and no longer about himself, he is able to move away from some of the self-mythologizing that went into the creation of *Gentleman Jigger*, a move which allows Nugent to explore more fully the absurdity of racialized thinking in a country where the lines demarcating the barriers between races becomes so amorphous as to be non-existent.

In *Half High*, the relationships that Aeon has with various people are foregrounded throughout the text. There are four important ones. First, his relationship with Beame, who is Black, although we only see her as a child, which puts them in a category somewhat beyond race; second, his relationship with Siempre, which is deeply neuroticized by the concept of race; third, his relationship with Shep, a white southern man, whose identity I am still not able to identify; and finally his relationship with Myra, or, following Tom Wirth, Dorothy Peterson, a Black writer who also hosted an important and influential literary salon during the Harlem Renaissance, although she is less well-known than some of the other Harlem Renaissance luminaries.

Another important difference in this novella is that, unlike *Infants of the Spring* and *Gentleman Jigger*, there is no attempt to pretend that the events in the story have any relation to actual events. By writing from the perspective of another member of the Harlem Renaissance, and one of the most mysterious of them at that, Nugent allows himself to use the techniques of fiction to drive home the points he is trying to make about the fluidity of race, gender and sexuality without getting trapped in the pitfalls of autobiographical writing.

Aeon's double consciousness allows him to understand that essentially questions of identity are meaningless, even though they paradoxically determine the meaning of everything one experiences in the United States. This leads to a series of relationships in which Blackness and whiteness are fused, but never quite come together; they become something of a chiaroscuro, in which the black and the white help define each other in relation and in contrast to each other. Nugent, in his visionary reimagining of the life of Jean Toomer, has created a unique work of Black modernism that finally finds its place in the literary world almost a hundred years after its conception.

Whit Frazier
Stuttgart, Germany
September 2023

HALF HIGH

Half-high they come, the Harlem Host Father, Son and Holy
Ghost –
(unholy Host) People pale (and dusky white)
Spawn of those so black as night

(and white) Flaunting black blood in white races Furtive-proud of
both their races
(Silly graces): Yea Half High the Harlem Host Father, Son and
Holy Ghost
Subtly smiles the while they're spending White regrets at Harlem
ending.
(Tomorrow pending)

1.   HALF HIGH
in which the world is begun and God in the first
person dies in child birth . . .

2.   EPISTLE
in which is explained how this all came to be . . .

3.   FATHER
in which Jesus is born and FATHER dies . . .

4.   SON
in which Jesus is educated and it proves fatal . . .

5.   --and HOLY GHOST
in which the ills of the world have been doctored
and the patient lives . . .

SEVEN AND . . .

I am Aeon Brennan. I am seven years old and a Negro. Am one of three minors who are the children of two adults who are the children each of two who are each the children of two. And they also. And more. I am Negro despite and because of my parents who are each the children of two, who are maybe-Negro and maybe-Nordic, each of whom are children of Nordic and Negro maybe. I am a Negro despite and because of my hazel eyes and white skin on slender hand, arm, body and foot. And lips . . . twin pale, thinly questions beneath the affirmation of narrow nostrils. I have a family. Three minors of whom I am but one pale slender contortion of questions meaning Negro. Despite and because my brothers are one and one. And each is yet grown pale in skin on hand, area, body and foot, being with family as an I. That there be dark under pale thoughts is as there is blood under skin. And we each are but one. Even encompassing the parents who are pale and dark with parents who are pale or dark with parents who are pale and pale and dark and dark.

I am, then, the impurities implying fusion. Which means weaknesses and strengths.

Which means strong weaknesses and weak strengths. We are these, then, and so we are Negro despite and because of pale skin covering slender hands, arms, bodies and feet, with pale under dark thoughts. And pale dark thoughts. And emotions. Even so am I. I am Aeon Brennan. I am seven years old and a Negro.

*****

I am playing with my cousin. My cousin is a girl and we are playing. Catherine. But with names are my thoughts, or if they be emotions, with names are my emotions aggravated. I cannot play with Catherine, so her name becomes Beama. It is a made name.

Beama is as female child as I am as male. Beama is of pale skin on slender beauty. Beama is Negro despite and because of two parents who are Negro each despite and because of two who are Negro and Nordic maybe and Nordic and Negro maybe who are the children of Negro and Negro maybe and Nordic and Nordic maybe. Beama is, despite and because, my playmate.

We are playing under the table. Playing at milking-the-sow. Milking-the-cow is a game which is played without play. I am the cow. No, I am the father and Beams is the mother. Only we are each the father and the mother. So we call the game, milking-the-cow. We have not yet discovered that a father is because of a mother. So I am the father. Or the mother. Beama is the mother, or the father. We are the father and the mother. Or the mother, depending on which of us like a mother is. Today Beama is. And being is, Beama is the mother as we sit under the table, hidden by the folds of a white square draped from the round surface above us. The littered white square of tablecloth holding crumbs and plates with crossed knives and forks over breakfast stains, and glasses with pale rings made by once-fresh milk. Over all of which are flies. And we sit under the table playing milking-the- cow, while the black shoes and stockings and edge of gingham skirt become the hired girl, walking to the table from the kitchen and to the kitchen from the table.

Milking-the-cow is a game which we play without play. Beama being the mother and I being the father, she is my wife but my mother as I am her husband but her father while we play a game without play not knowing that Beama is as female to me who is as male.

Differences of anatomy become discoveries which become knowledge of differences. I, being the father, discover me to be deformed. For I have appendages which add no beauty to me as the lack in Beama is beauty. So we are curious. Beama is the mother but a child who is more practical, and thinks not beauty nor disfiguration of beauty as do I who am a child but the father. To Beama useful is beauty, as different from me, beauty being useful. So Beams caresses with pale skin of hand the disfigurement of me as compared to the sweet curve of line making for beauty in her body, pale in slender unbroken line from toe to head. Because I am in profile after caresses, a line broken below the torso to be continued. Beama caresses that which, as I stand, breaks with pale horizontal my line of contour which if one closes an eye, is as hers, and hence to me, beauty. So Beama caresses pale horizontal and we are curious.

So curious that we are all unaware of else save the beauty of difference. And that there is no longer the shield to our play formed by the drape of a square of white cloth over the surface above us. And my mother smacks our hands and arranges our clothes and tells us we must not do that. Despite the fact that I tell her that Beama is the mother and I am the father and we are playing a game called milking-the-cow, which is a game to be played without play. She says instead that Beama is not Beama but Catherine and not the mother but cousin and that I am not the father but Aeon and her cousin. She will not hear me say that I am the father with broken line of beauty. She says that we are too young to play the game of milking-the-cow.

But I know better. And I know that Beama knows. And that Beama is never again Catherine but Beama. But I am curious. For there is more than empty to other games: Except this one which is only empty. And why does pale horizontal break darkly the line of vertical me, making for unlike the vertical of Beama? Also, if there is that which I am to discover, why am I told not to discover? That is not beautiful.

Beauty is beauty. Beauty and beauty is beauty and . . . And more. Ugly is beauty.

Beauty is. Despite, and in, or apart of ugly. Even better. Beauty encompasses ugly. I know. Even though I am seven and the palely son of two who are each one of two maybe-dark, maybe-pale who are each one of two maybe-dark-pale-and-pale-dark who are each one of two maybe-dark-and-dark and maybe-pale-and-pale. Through, and up to, and because of me they are beauty also. For I am beauty. Beauty encompasses even so.

*****

Because of family growing greatly and multiple from my mother through my father, I go to live in Beama's home. And so I grow to know less of my brother who is Stuartt and is younger and my brother who is Rhythm and is youngest. And this is no hurt to me, for we are, even though like, very different. I am different in my ways as is each of my brothers and so we are not hurt. For each of us is in great magnitude individual. And knows not the other. So we do not feel the separation and do not too often see each other.

But I grow to love with great love my mother who, through instinct knowing so completely, is well aware and with love and sympathy if not understanding for and of me. And I grow to love with great love my father of whom I am a greater part. And his slow smile and gentle voice is with me long after his visits to me are over and his smile remains with me as do his words long after his each departure.

And my mother. Mother is to me eternal and love becomes awesome in its magnitude. For she visits me often likewise. And is as my mother. And I love her also even more. For mother is possessed of great strength and is always with me. And always with Beama although we see her more seldom. We love mother.

*****

I grow and am more than seven. I grow and in growing am more. That is as should be. I still play. Because to play is to play without playing. That is if I play at the certain things. I do. And others.

And with others. With others also. That I am as the others who are also the children of two who are no longer pale and pale or dark and dark is significant. I am as they. So with them only must I play and talk and later talk aid love, love and marry and procreate. That is simple. There is no reason given for that. I am too young to understand. Or if I am not too young, it is needless to explain. It is a thing that I must grow knowing and believing as I grow knowing and believing in Jesus, books and mother. That I should grow knowing means that if I have thoughts that are not just the thoughts to have, then must I pretend not to have them. That is not right. That is play. That is the play that one plays playing. The things which I must not do are the things that interest me more. They are the things at which I can play without play.

An errand to the washerwoman to ask her with polite "please" to call for the clothes is to play. There are at the house of the washerwoman many things to which Beama and I are strangers. So Beama laughs and it is a laugh that would be loud because mother is not near to say hush. Only it is not loud because mother is still with us although we are now two blocks from where we left her. Mother is always with us. Unless we pretend. I am a manchild and have been taught that men are not afraid. So I laugh and it is a laugh that is louder. But not loud yet. Because mother is still with us. And I am not yet as unafraid as I shall be. Beama laughs at my laugh. And hers is now loud save in beauty. I laugh and my laugh borrows beauty from my fear. But it is not beauty. Yet Beama laughs and it is good. It has grown in beauty like a song. And we laugh beauty loud and loud. And it is beauty even more. It is the beauty that announces us who are beauty to the washerwoman who is as ugly. And being as ugly is even beauty. We come close to the door. There is a nice nigger-smell. Nigger-odor. Like closed bureau drawers thrown open after mice have lain there. And there is musk. And there is herself.

She is black with the blackness that Beama and I must not know. With the black like the soft black contralto voice. There is deep purple in her blackness. And on her forehead are many globes of sweat that hold the black end purple of her in their moist spheres like opals . . . There is the room in which she stands over the tub. It is a kitchen and is perfumed with the forbidden nigger-odor. And there are children.

A little girl with black-brown skin on a too-perfect body. With bead-black eyes that are enhanced by her half-closed lids heavy with laughter. Her hair is short. So short that it merely meets as tiny crests between the many parts. And on these crests is the color, the green brown color of licorice bitten through.

And a boy. A boy with legs that are twin curves of black that hold purple in slender contortion. And lips that pout above a chin that nearly is not and thereby furnishes the point to the oval-in-all-ways-an-oval that is his head.

These then and even these as playmates are forbidden. Because they hold laughter as a feather. And life as a breath to juggle laughter on. Because eyes can grow thin with laugh and fat with tears and fat with laugh and thin with tears. And be changing beauty. Thin-fat-laugh-tears-beauty to color even breaths, feathers and the kitchen, being to the washerwoman life, and hence, of her.

And ever because we are one, Beama and Aeon, meaning one and one only one, we grow love. And because there is love between us, ever growing tall like a thin curve of never-ending, we are one. Despite love between us and because love between us is. And so high and so high, while so wide and so wide that we are one and one. Even so and because we are one and one, with this love between us, we are only one. Ever we fertilize this love with the beauty of black line of beauty made yet more beauty because of red. Beama loves as I love, not only these and me, but because of these and me. And even the love itself for itself. And doing so causes yet more love in and of me, even as I cause by the same token yet more love in and of her. And so the growth in one makes more startling the growth in yet one which does likewise. And there is a beginning.

*****

We yet play without play at more and the same things. There is "amen" in the Baptist Church despite polite and paler rituals Presbyterian. Or Episcopalian. Beama and I steal the Baptist amen along with weird beauties of dissonant fervor to love between and through each other. Despite solemn Episcopalian "ave maria" and holy communion. Because Baptist flings unwanted rhythm and startling loudnesses to encompass God in forbidden glory.

Because beads of sweat make unfamiliar sounds and smells to accompany with beauty the amen rising from pendulous sacred hung lips dripping with song in many unrepeated harmonies. And there are fingers that reach heaven in massed upthrown individual ecstasy above feet that shuffle song-sounds as they deeper sink roots into earth. Beauty of bodies giving vent between extreme of finger and foot, to religious fervor, through sex orgies.

Revelation of the impossible greatness of belief that more than spans the discrepancies between earth and sky.

There is Miss Veasy who is official midwife and wet nurse. Miss Veasy is also to be absorbed, because she is all that is forbidden save in place designed by parents, meaning only is she useful being midwife and wet nurse. But she is also the teller of tales. And lives alone with magic and voodoo unknown on a high hill, alone. Only do Beama and I discover that she has for company unseen souls and unheard sounds.

Her thick pendulous lips sag at the end of tired jowl muscles, their weight causing a pucker under half closed tired eyes. Eyes tired with the seeing of babies born and unseen souls she sees. There are bags under her eyes. Green-yellow bags. When she smiles the strain caused by heavy lips make wrinkles at the corner of eyes. She is big-framed and yellow-skinned, and fat sags in expected places more than is expected. Her voice is a high, heavy drawl passing through lips too tired with their own weight to move much. Her voice always drops before she has completed her words, and they hang heavily in the air from almost visible threads through her lips, from the too-tired and puckered eyes. And she is, despite and because, beauty to be absorbed. She is a teller of tales. She tells us that we love. And to Beama and me that is vision.

So we grow. And in growing are more. And I grow. And in growing draw life completely from my father. Or so it seems. He dies and all life ceases. Even love for Beama ceases. For in dying has my father cut from me a source of my growing.

*****

And I am older now that my father is dead. Am older and only one of three who are each possessed by mother. Curiosities of sex become sex and I am with Beama curious. I am now twelve years old and have discovered that there are to be had pleasures to be arrived at through the medium of self. It is an amazing discovery. There is also fear, the pleasure is so intense. There is also Beama. With Beama now do differences become obstacles to be overcome. With me are they existing to be first enjoyed through learning than learned through enjoyment. We are still young enough to be allowed to sleep together. And soft in the night do I fondle the soft strangeness of near beauties in the contour of Beama, that are as pale cups of firm flesh inverted. As in contrast to the hard bareness of my own chest.

Because of the soft tautness of her breasts do I find new pleasures in the hard structure of the clean sweep of straightness that is my body above the waist. No longer are we as like. Rather are we growing to be more perfect complements one to the other. Dark rests as closely on me as does the caress of the soft of Beama beside me. And she is with head turned towards me breathing slowly and slightly. The warmth of her breath perfumes the pleasant contact of our thighs and calves. Softly, with timid hands grown hot with boldness of unlearned desire, fingers mold contours as contact is assured. Lips held on lips by weak breaths sobbing with the knowledge of knowing through consummation. I am frightened by the too-strong pleasure and lie faintly in the calm mystery of Beama. She is smiling invisibly. And I weep. Only there is also courage in my tears.

There are soft rhythms of well-being. And there is Beama and the dark and me. And all are one, in and because of and through the other and each other.

So there grows greater, between Beama and me, love that can through consummation be even love again.

It is morning and I lie with my face warm with sun. On my back and with one knee drawn up and my other leg full length spread against the warm space between Beama and me. There is more than just morning or sun. There is warm space between Beama and me though between us.

Beama opens her eyes and there are caresses that tangibly entangle with soft suddenness the lazy beauty I had been enjoying. And there are fingers to prove through unconscious fondling that there is more to this also than empty. I love Beama.

CHIAROSCURO

Living in New York is no different. And yet living in New York is all change. So I work and have still a family which possesses a hired girl who has each Thursday free. And I have friends who enjoy as I enjoy. The only difference being in having longer been. They are all pale of skin; but the paley children of two who were Nordic and Nordic, who were the children each of two who were Nordic and Nordic who were each the children of two who were Nordic and Nordic. Maybe. Only am I different in being the child of two who were Nordic and Negro, maybe, who were each the child of two who were Negro and Nordic. That I have, through being of white skin on arm, neck and foot, become white is that I have, despite being Negro, relinquished even my race. And with all the exquisite agony of being beautiful as what I was, to become even beautiful as what I now, being other, am. I am now Nordic. Transition of status is not difficult to accomplish when one is with family as am. I. Nor is transition of race startling, being merely change from one like to like of another race. Like, being the conduct and actions of middle-class America.

Living in New York and being white is no different. Even am I fairer of skin and with lighter eyes than most of my associates. I am more than twenty-one years old and no longer feel that New York is a stranger, but a friend of many facets. I no longer feel that my white friends should think other than white and white. No longer do I weep or walk many hours through the night because Beama has died.

Only do I feel how sad that now I cannot marry her but only love her. How sad that I was not near to pretend not to notice the disagreeable odor surrounding her illness. For before she died of consumption she had also catarrh and was unpleasant to smell. And could not understand. But I who lived and was loving her would have been always with her.

Nothing in my living is changed. We have a hired girl who has Thursdays free. We go to theatres and buy ready-made, clothes. We have friends. For mother who is young is still attractive attracted. She has remarried and we are provided with a new father. Rather am I provided with a new father. For Stuartt has left us and traveled to Spain. And we know that we shall never be as family to him again.

And Rhythm has likewise withdrawn. And become a dancer. And Mother and I know that we shall be all the family there is. For neither Stuartt nor Rhythm will return. They have remained Negro and we have remained white. And never again shall I, as in greater childhood, have my brothers as brothers.

My mother's husband is a publisher and collector of rare books. I have a position with him. And freedom both economic and social. Again I am aware of no great fundamental change.

Because of certain social abilities I become the "contact" member of my step-father's firm. I have my separate quarters.

At a party for an author whom we desire to place under contract I meet Siempre. And since we are by each even more than attracted, she comes to live with me.

Siempre's hair is three colours. Dark brown on either side of the part. Then reddish. Auburn. But where she brushes it back over her ears it is gold-almost-silver. That is why I love her. And. she is a painter of growing fame. Because her teeth are far apart she is beautiful. Because her ankles are slim she is good. And she has three children and no husband. She is twenty-seven years old. Six years older than I.

And I meet Shep. He is tall, slow, Southern and white. This attraction is for me so great and emotional that it is almost androgynous. It is strange that this antithesis to everything safe should arouse me so emotionally. I feel strangely that I cannot encompass quite the importance of this meeting. It is an intangible feeling. Everyone who knows Shep laughingly calls him The Genius. And I find myself not laughing as I also think of him as The Genius. For me there is a touch of the divine, the too-intense surrounding him. I find him a place in my stepfather's business. And through him I grow.

Frequently am I embarrassed by his regard for me. I become ashamed of the androgynous sense he exudes and makes me conscious of. For it is definitely not homosexuality. It is that sexless greatness and love that apostles of beauty, prophets of the immortal liveness, alone exude. And I try to capture it, catalogue it, personalize it.

*****

My first love was after my second. As on Sunday morning while with various practices erotic occupied there all the while waft up to us the pale sounds of episcopal worship from the church below. There is the pale hymn to be joined in ascension by soft kisses of Siempre and me in passing. My second love was prior to my first. Siempre lies beside me soft breathing into my ear and lips greater love than can I in return impart. For through Siempre am I even yet in love and more than greatly with my first love. And that is to be accepted no matter how strange for I was not until now really in love ever.

The hymn from below rises to a phallic point as we two in bed above reach climax to be told in sobbing sighs from lip to lip in kissing. Beama now has become a criterion with which to perfume all fundamentals emotional and sexual. Even as I sit in a chair and before and beside me stands Siempre bending forward to kiss with passion and with love again my forehead, as her breasts brush blue blown whiteness of soft pendant coral nippled desire against the firm favor of my too-willing lips. And I am consumed even more by the casual contact of thigh calf and toe until with arms grown adept through longing I carry her to the bed and we are again through each other even love, while the canting of "Father, Son and Holy Ghost, Amen" softs through the vibrant moon-shade of her hair I have hidden us with.

We sit at breakfast and I think that it is strange that I should find my love for Siempre growing greater because I have discovered that she is to be loved by me only through Beama. And through Beams is she made yet more beautiful and am I allowed to love her even yet more. Then there was more than just love for Beama. There was also permanent greatness. And beauty. Beauty that can by having been make yet more beauty. Beama is as a filter through which all things to reach me in the full import of their beauty must pass. And yet am I also in love with Siempre because she is Siempre and I feel that only I can love with such completeness. Only I am with fragile strength great enough to dare to be even too full or empty entirely. And yet full.

*****

An elevated crashes overhead shattering all my thoughts with noise. Making them spread in circles. Then larger circles like a splash in a pool. Of what had I been thinking?

Death. Or without life at least. But death. In spreading circles: circles making larger circles and all life affected because of death. Like a splash in a pool. A sky is held up on converging rows of roofs, and punctured with star-points.

> "Night now breathes a syllabled rune,
> And the fawn wraith beckons me:
> So I follow the wraith up to the moon
> Over a silver path on the sea.

(This thought I leave to cover you
As sunshine covers shade—
To hold you in the personal way
That mountains hold a glade:)
I think that it is best by far
That you remember me
As climbing down to aid a star
Drowned in a night drunk sea."

There breaks around me now, like a shower, the activities of more happy creatures. Like a deluge the fact of not being, nor yet not being not. And there is no midway even though I walk it. There is only not being that which I, nor even that which I am not. Not being even the thing I am for fear that, through being, I will then become not at all. Are there many, many of us who die and yet live after we are dead?

I am dead. And yet in being even dead do I live more cruelly. Even more. I am not. Nor have I ever been. Nor can I be Negro. Nor can I be Nordic. Nor can I be that cameleopard Aframerican. I can only be as . . . Sunshine covers shade. And all of the weird change in me be even me because I am not. I walk slow music through the streets of New York, and am myself even the slow music which I walk. And that will be forever. I am afraid. So I recognize my fear. And like a dervish, whirl in never ending circles with pain pins through my flesh of soul. And yet I am only half high.

Only am I half high behind lips, twin, pale, thinly questions grown tight and firm to hold back black blood with a white skin. And only am I half high behind Nordic restraint grown brittle with holding back Negro rhythms. Pale thought oppressing dark emotions like frayed ivory over light. Like sunshine covers shade. And I walk slow music into Harlem.

It is my first time in Harlem. One-Hundred-and-Thirty-Third Street. Beale Street.

Beale Street is the sound center of Harlem. And I walk slow music. In a cabaret the dancers move without sound to the rhythm of the underpulse of drums. Or do they? Each movement of hip is a vibrating boom from the tom-tom I hear with my bowels. The sound of the drum is pitched at just the depth to reverberate in the bowels. A pleasant thrilling pulsing between the hips. And the clarinet weaves a minor treble that titulates in my throat and quivers on my lips. The saxophone drawls off beat harmonies that quicken with monotony and fascination my abdominal regions to syncopation. And the kettle drum and trombone teach slow intricacies to my sensitive and no longer uncertain feet. I dance with an entertainer.

She is slender in her frail entirety of beauty as I am through one thigh. Soft in my arms, with straightened hair glossed to a blue highlight painted on my chest: I find myself swaying, in music. In, of, and through music. Rhythm is to be enjoyed even closely with feet merely to accompany body movements. And too soon the dance is over and my partner says to me, "Gee, you must a been in Harlem a lot. You dance almos' as good as a cullud fella."

And I walk afterwards, South, which is from Harlem. And I think that perhaps my theory is wrong. That perhaps I place in ascendance that which should not be. All life affected by my death? Is it not so that reversed the thought may to me mean more?

All death affected by my life. My thoughts become as fourth-dimensional. And time is not. Nor space. Nor time-space. No longer am I non-existent. Merely am I always. Even before, and now, and after. After being future, before being past, now being present. And all being but a continuity of one. And that one, being but yet a part of another many of which make for something more nearly a whole. I, being of three dimensions in thought, see only as through a telescope through which is visible merely that part of me on which I focus. And that section of my vision I name past, as this I name present, and the other I name future.

Only I focus a blurred vision on that which is before me and cannot see with the clarity with which I view the other two. Since the future then is but of the fourth-dimensional solidity which is me, being the name I choose to give men, being yet only a part of the whole I call animal, being but a part of even evolution, and the whole being an inert solidity, I can if I want, focus more clearly on the part of the whole, the future of me, and see that of which I am curious. And my vision when thus focused tells me merely that the future is as the past and that I am not as a whole, more than a minute part. I am to me the most important of all parts, however. So I plumb the future, to find it slipping back into the present into the past as I focus yet more ahead. Even then was my second love prior to, or simultaneous with, my first.

Reduced to such finite conceptions, nothing I do or am matters. And though I am by this thought burdened with regret at my unimportance, so also am I lightened. And I shall no longer try to belong to a race of which I am only a part, nor shall I refute my other parts.

Rather shall I speak and experiment even with my own love. And examine my own hurt. So I reach home.

Siempre sits and folds her love into my lips as I kiss her. "Siempre, do you love me so that my being part Negro does not matter?" And Siempre barricades her love behind an incredulous laugh and says, "Are you joking, Aeon?"

So, as I light a cigarette and can feel a sickening tightening in my stomach, I think: I am being vain to be afraid, and being afraid and yet more afraid of being afraid I say, "But I am a Negro despite being as many parts white as black. Or red and yellow maybe."

And she answers, "Oh, I see. But if we all trace back that far we are all bleak and white, or red or yellow maybe." And her voice drifts on to protoplasms. To which I calmly furnish an insane objection for her to use against me.

"You see, Siempre, I mean my father was part Negro and my mother, and their fathers and their mothers maybe. And I have no argument with their choice to love. I am their offspring."

And Siempre looks long at me, closing nearly her slender eyes. Then she reaches for a cigarette, lights it and blows a large cloud of smoke before she speaks.

"Do you mean you're a nigger?" And her voice is as slow and thin as the smoke from her cigarette. I do not answer. Why am I telling her this? How should she act? I watch her as she inhales and exhales. She speaks:

"I wouldn't mind if you were black. I'd like to have an affair with a black man." She laughs slightly. ". . . to even have a child for a black man. To see his black against my white and feel him and know he was a nig-Negro. If you were white I'd marry you. I love you. If you were black I'd go to bed with you. And maybe love you. But if I'm going to love a nigger, he has to be a nigger and if I love a white man he must be white."

And I, who had known all the while that this would be the way it would happen, am hurt inside. I curl up and am ill inside at every word. I speak and my voice is as it always was:

"I am sorry, Siempre, that not being black I am insufficient as a lover, and not being white, am inadequate as a husband. I am also sorry that being a mixture of both you cannot see me as complete. And yet I'm very glad. Because there are things I must know—even this sadness. The next time I go to Harlem I shall remain."

But my words sound hollow. I shall remain if I can. I know they sound strange to Siempre also for she looks at me and speaks, saying, "I shall leave you, Aeon, but there is no need to become colored, no need to forfeit all that you have gained. I shall never tell, because I loved and love you. Why bother? Why not let's go on? No one will ever know and we can be happy."

Then when everything is here within my grasp I turn all aside by saying, "What if the child is colored?"

Siempre is gone. Beama through Siempre is gone. And I, who was built so well to be am no longer. There is no need to make display of my color. Just to drop out of the lives of my friends and family. And if ever I meet with them in Harlem, they will know when they see me with the Negroes I shall discover. For I am of the chameleon race. I am saying happy things but I am alone. I am no longer a child and can now face myself and know—know that with whites my lack of color leaves me white. And with Negroes my blood shows through my skin and I am as they. I turn again to Harlem.

TWENTY AND TWO

Long sad streets like funeral wails. Punctuated with pale sad people. Night spills softly around me in a melancholy drape, hiding perfumed sorrows in the memory folds. A sad gray city erected by a contrite God to wall and prison me in confines so stifling that the infinite be no longer unobtainable. The infinite, welling above and around me in tangible grayness and futility. Promises of ashes cast flagrantly upon a perverse and drab breeze that cloys my face and gags my lungs until my senses reel and with a triple burst stagger from my nostrils. All emotions enter in and became a part of the melancholy greatness around me. No longer am I cloyed with ashes of tears wept for a color-spasm of love or grief. I am about to become great in my smallness and inhale into my being, like a hasheesh dream of pain, all the drabness of a gray infinity. All the satiation of lackcolorness, when . .

Music screams a void somewhere between the bent sky and beveled pavement. And night hangs black around the hollow. Raucous music making a vacuum of lighted hollows rimmed in coherent and awed silence. Catching an occasional vulgar laugh and hoisting its shrill tone until, puncturing the raucous music, it spills with tense metallic trickles over the edge, into the silence.

Grayness broken into myriads of hopeless bits. Turning suddenly colors to be absorbed. To bite into me. To be inhaled with the finite back through reluctant nostrils to lungs weary with brutal efforts. Stabbing my consciousness with pain of inhalation of water. Drowning. Filling my lungs with stinging fluid. Smarting my eyes with peacock liquid. Pain. Scarlet and vivid. Embodying in itself the many colors too painful to bear. Then soothing —cool —and the gray grows dimmer through a translucent moon.

God walking Lenox Avenue swinging a can can well laugh. Heels be-come a symbol of buried gray as I sink unconscious back into a hell of colors waters too deep mount and dot with black the smiling yellow eyes of yellow whores. Mouths like a disease beckon and smile with thirty-two teeth and hips. A silk ankle is a slender blown line enticing God to masturbation as he stands with one hand in a pocket, twirling a cane and watching me lewdly slough into the footsteps of some whore's pimp.

"Say, buddy, got a match?"

I give him one and he lights a cigarette and stands beside smoking. I am sullen with frustration. As though I were apart from me I can see us standing there. Hear us passing remarks on women that pass. A yellow poured into transparent hose and a dark dress is a girl. I would like to know her.

"Sure," she lays. "I'll take you." And, my friend guides me up Seventh Avenue. Into a dark side street. Then up three flights of stairs that creak and groan under the weight of worn and broken linoleum. He knocks a signal at a worn door. After a rattling of chains and throwing of bolts the door is cracked and we are admitted into a narrow hall lit with a dull red bulb. Then into a room filled with smoke and dull lights and smells. Sex-exciting body smells. I sit on a couch and the yellow girl whom we had followed comes in and sits beside me. . The madam brings us gin. Dollar Harlem gin. She tosses hers off with a snort. I turn to the yellow girl and soon our bodies become warm and fetid with contact and more gin. Her lips are formless and wet. We go into another room. In bed we toss and storm. I am sated.

Sweat runs down from my neck and makes wet sucking under my chest between her breasts. Organic smells well from our loins and bellies, and intoxicate me. A breeze cools the sweat on my buttocks and the damp back of my calves when she unlocks. And I lie spent, her breath more languid than mine. Finally I slide away and lie with eyes closed breathing regularly between the sheets. Long and satisfied. She softly leaves the bed. From beneath half-closed eyelids I can see her running deft fingers through my pants pockets without disturbing their folded position on the chair. I speak. She stiffens, then brazenly turns.

"You Goddamn white bastard!"

*****

There is a day beginning. And hard straight streets. There is an empty Seventh Avenue. Noises are each separate from the other. Are individual and material because there is a still aftermath of a noise-filled night. I shove my shirt more firmly under my belt and am sober. Clear. And with a desire for a population where there is only an empty Seventh Avenue. A disturbance. Anything. My cigarette smoke mounts erect to a thinness. Someone running behind me only helps make the street seem more silent with the clatter of feet.

"Yeah. That's him, the Goddamn bastard!" sounds from around the abrupt corner I had turned. I face about. A glimpse of the yellow girl, then the crash of a fist against my mouth. Flattening my lips painfully against my teeth. My lips tear and my head cracks against the pavement. I am dizzy. I get to one knee, my hand pressed against my bloodied lips. My feet are on the ground again and I unbend. A thud somewhere in my head and a throbbing on my left cheek, then my nose and mouth flattened against a fist again. All I see is blood-shot eyes in black. And hear a grunt from the impact in a brown suit. Again my shoulders jar on the asphalt. A thud in the ribs.

"Leave our women alone, you damn . . ."

And another kick. For a while I just lie there taking a strange pleasure in my throbbing body and pulsing lips.

"Goddamn white bastard!"

Then I get up, dusting myself off and with head throbbing and ribs aching, walk on down Seventh Avenue. I am happy. Only bothered that my lips sting when I try to pucker them to whistle. But the tune dances on ahead of me. Noisy and vulgar. Like a yellow girl in transparent hose. I am content.

The subway is a black twisting rush of breeze. Whipping around me. Slapping my trousers against my calves and running swift disarranging fingers through my hair. A black twisting rush of breeze splashed with furious streaks of light. Swallowing me, the train, and its contents with implacable indiscretion. Inevitably growing from a never-dying point, to a round full-ness embracing a noisy clattering light that wheels on and on into the deathless point. Trailing off into an ever near and constant, yet swiftly diminishing, perspective. All of us and me held with calm inevitability in the vortex of this rushing black. What would the all-unaware people think, if they knew I was rushing to suicide because I am colored, only am I so well white that I can never be colored? Would God know that I did not believe in Him? That this was to me a symptom of defiance? Soon there would be fewer hiatuses in this roaring black. Fewer white platforms on which to ejaculate people with the unconcern of a whorehouse keeper. Soon I would be loosed on a white platform and read Battery Park. Perhaps I should be reviewing my past life or must I wait until the agony of drowning gives place to a soothing somnambulistic feeling. So to drown, then have my life unreel before comfortable and impersonal eyes. I can't do that. Yet how can I be any way but impersonal. I will be comfortable. Will have the knowledge that nothing matters. That everything will cease to be when I cease to be. I will be too aware of my juxtaposition to existence for it to matter. But my very awareness may call forth a reel of theory. Vital theory. As vital as all life is while one lives. Life is theory. Maybe it is not. But at least I will be able to indulge in a finer way my love for that state which is neither sleep nor wakefulness. And in that state, thumb my nose at God standing on the prow of a tug thinking about the girls I did not know. God, smiling lewdly, that I should be trying to make a gesture, leave him a clean sweep for an experienced man. God is incapable of appreciating a gesture.

*****

I have wandered around all day. It is growing late in Battery Park now. The softening green becoming gray. This slapping blue becoming gray. These benches inhabited becoming gray, and pouring into me and becoming more gray and almost black. This lull of color tacked down by yellow lights for me to see. By the softened and startling screams of boat whistles and moving lights over slapping gray becoming more gray. A soft lilt of tune floating over and through this colorlessness to become part of it and soften it even as it becomes softened by it. All of this making empty feelings to pour into me. Into the void of me and fill with void the void within me. Dull red of brick felt through gray. Because I am aware that its color is red. Only it is gray. And each is true. Truth cannot be. Truth must be relative. I refute cabalism. That truth is. Reconcile for me that red is gray. It is so simple. As simple as the fact that I was going to thumb my nose at God by dying and do it now instead by living. By letting the soft red or brick, the brilliant clash of green, the lilting light of blue, all pour into me as gray. Each in itself gray. All combined, gray. And empty. As full as this gray must be, it is empty. And pours into me who am empty. And fills me with emptiness. I know nothing. Not even that I know I know nothing. I believe nothing. All this —? It is called the world. Myself? Am I? Color —? They say. But is it —? I do not know. I believe —? I cannot say. Why —? Because I do not know. I do not have to know to believe? Belief is not knowledge . . . I am only aware. Of what? That I know and believe I may not know and believe and I may and may not and yes is no and no is yes and yes is if and no is if and if is may and may is yes and yes is may and may is no and no is may and may is not and may not is may . . .

To have a conceit let God or maybe not God listen or maybe not while I speak or maybe not to a man or maybe not who speaks to me or maybe not and says or maybe not that he or maybe not wants or maybe not a match. Or maybe not. And I or maybe not give it or maybe not to him or maybe not. How complicated. Or maybe not. So you live in the village. He has spoken or maybe not and I answer yes. Or maybe not. And in our conversation if there were one (was there?), he (or is he) asks (or does he) (or is he) do I (if I am) know Siempre I (if I am) (am I) answer maybe (or maybe not). I (if I am) do (possibly). And he (if he is) calls her (if she is) a whore but a virgin. And I (if I am) know (or maybe not) that she (if she is) a whore (if a whore is) and a virgin (if a virgin is). I (if I am) explain or maybe not. And our conversation, if there were one, has progressed beyond my thought (or has it) for I say (or do I) (if I am) but she has hallucinations. And he answers, hallucinations? Say what the hell do you think she is?

So I just sit and think, and wish to smoke while I sit and think, that once I was seven years old and of course born and that at one time my thoughts that I now remember still are although they were when I was seven and so they were and are even though I am no longer seven years old but more and, therefore, still seven and eight and all the years and months and weeks and days and hours and minutes and seconds between then and now including even before then through and up until now. Even am I still twelve when my father died and I felt strange because nothing seemed strange not even that father should die or that I not think it strange or weird even though it was night with one blue end yellow gas-flame flickering and making Mother seem weird and frightened while she seemed so the same as though at some time it must have happened before, and I knew even then that nothing happens in the present because the past registers what was the present happening on my mind instead of the present making its impress in the present just as now I am even while thirteen much more and remember my emotions when I was thirteen and then in the present of the time which is now past and was never present because I never lived it in the present except to say this-and-this is happening now only, by the time I thought it, it was past and always will be past by the time I receive it. Past, present and future can only be marked as a stream divided in three by strings held under the water and one part flows into the other and is not really divided. I get up from the bench in Battery Park and walk to the elevated. I am glad I decided to thumb my nose at God by refusing to commit suicide. I wanted to too badly. God is incapable. I hire a small room on Washington Square because I remember that Siempre is no longer at home waiting. And I am too great a coward to return to depleted and unhappy quarters. I have no emotions. I am reading *Rhapsody, A Dream Novel.* In a room with a bed, a chair, a table, and a bilious bureau. Suddenly I become aware that I have been disturbed and annoyed for the last nineteen minutes by the blind flutterings of a moth. It becomes unbearable, I become frightened. Nervously I grab a towel and hit at the moth. My fear renders me inaccurate. I strike again. Again. And still this flurry of wings bumping, thudding against four walls, the door, a bed, a chair, a table, and a bilious bureau. I become frantic. I chase this fluttering fluttering. Then I strike it. A powdery streak is all that is left. I lie back down to read *Rhapsody, A Dream Novel.* And thoughts intrude unwanted. Maybe that moth was Jesus. Just like Jesus. To worry, harass me into noticing his blind dashes into the light. All becomes symbolic only that was really Jesus. Jesus with his flair for cheap theatrics. But the damn thing made me itch all over. Made me creep, made me feel unclean. And now. But that was Jesus. I have mashed Jesus. Why had I been so afraid of a moth with beautiful gray wings. With a soft whirring end a graceful swoop into light. To have killed it with my hands would have been awful. Would have been soft and wet. Would have stained. Why should I be possessed of such unreasoning fear of a moth? Unless it was Jesus. Jesus blindly leading me in fluttering circles. Leading me into futile blunderings against four walls, a chair, a door and a bilious bureau. It could not have been Jesus. I don't believe in Jesus. How can I believe in Jesus when I don't believe in God? Wasn't God the Father of Jesus? This Three in One.

Father, Son, and Holy Ghost. God must be an amoeba. The lowest form of life. An awful thing to know that millions of people kneel in millions of beautiful buildings to worship an amoeba. Why, in the cathedral at Toledo alone are hoarded fabulous beauties in precious stones and metals and cloths and materials. All dedicated, more consecrated, to the worship of an amoeba-. And worse. Myriads of beautiful boys, and by boys I mean eyelashes and eyes and lips and delicate throats, soft arms and legs immature and pathetically beautiful chests and loins, fingers that itch to play, and hair that smells vaguely of the inexpressible perfume of cleanliness and sweat —boys with wondrous silver voices, beautiful dreams and minds, all sacrificed to this voracious Amoeba. And girls. Long hair shorn, beauty of budding breast and rounding thigh, delicately turned ankle hidden under ugly habiliments. Eyes and lips that will never know and throats and arms that can never feel. All because of this amoeba. And I should believe in Jesus. In that myth for dependent minds. In that narcotic for: fear-pained souls. Afraid not to have something to blame, to thank, to ask of, to pray to, to worship and do for. I pick up another book. Hunger. It is raining outside. I am restless. I am sleepy. I want to go out in the rain. But I am sleepy. I undress. Turn off the light, stumble over the chair.

"Goddamn it!"

I kneel beside the bed. "Our Father, who art in heaven" . . . why in the name of hell am I praying? I don't believe in God! Habit, that's all. But I said "hell." I can't believe in hell either then. Just an expression . . . "Hallowed be Thy name." Why do I continue? Now I can't remember any more of it. How does it go? Maybe God is proving to me He does exist by this play with my memory. I will remember it just to prove to Him that He does not exist . . . "Thy kingdom come, Thy will be done" . . . There! I remembered even though You tried Your best . . . "On earth as it is in Heaven" . . . There is no such place . . . "Give us this day our daily bread and forgive us our trespasses as we forgive those who trespass against us" . . . If you really are God, You will certainly follow the teachings of Your own prayer

and forgive me for not believing in You . . . "Lead us not into temp-
tation, but deliver us from evil . . . For Thine is the Kingdom" . . .
Silly ritual . . . "the Power and the Glory for ever and ever, Amen."
Dear Lord, please forgive me for my thoughts about You. I climb
into bed. Why had I said all that? The last was not habit. And I don't
believe in God. How can any reasoning being do so? All this thought
over a silly moth. But the moth may have been Jesus. Couldn't have
been, because Jesus is not. I may have killed Jesus. Oh, God, if I —I
couldn't have killed Him for He is not. Sounds biblical. I'm so sleepy.
Please God let me sleep.

But I cannot sleep. I leave my hired room.

*****

And so I return. No longer to live out of the possible. But back to
my quarters And on my right there is light, on my left there is Jesus.
But on my right there is light. Once I had seen a whore grow all
yellow in the flicker of a gas flame . . . I once went home with a
whore: And as we went through the streets she was beautiful. Up two
flights. Noisy stairs.

Then a small room smelling of bodies. Many stale body odors.
And cheap perfume and gas. And soiled linen and closed bureau
drawers. I struck a match and she guided my hand to the gas jet.
Then I saw all I had smelled. All except the many bodies. As she
undressed she coughed. Her underwear was clean, rough-dry. And
soon she lay before me. But I was sick. The promise of luscious
brown proved to be a faded yellow. Worn gold. She saw me as I
made an involuntary effort to rebutton my clothes. Her eyes became
large. In that moment she knew and dreaded life. I kissed her on the
forehead and felt like Jesus. I felt it all again. And in the night I felt
like Jesus . . . All saints and holy men were criminals. But it was nice
to feel saintly end criminal like Jesus. Jesus and I walked hand in
hand.

And so I reach my quarters. And as I undress I know that Siempre
has returned.

There is an odor in the rooms that can only be through the presence of Siempre. And from the dark she speaks and says, "We love each other, Aeon, and I have come. And long we sleep in the comfort of love for each other."

ETIOLATED

Siempre and I decide. And New York becomes a point of starting.
We go to Taos.

And live.

To live in Taos with Siempre is to be happy. I have learned that I do love Siempre. There are long days of only love. And there are days of work. I am now a poet. I now write many poems that are with more meaning fraught than I know.

Long purple covers our content and we are in love. Always there is the solace of Siempre-lips. For I do need solace. And I forget that there is other than as I now am. There has never been other except as a vague dream to remember and to cherish with pale and beautiful melancholy.

I sit naked save for many turquoise beads and believe poetry. Because turquoise beads make more gold and white the lie that is me. Hide more securely a mongrel and passionate parentage. And there are guests for whom I don a robe of feathers given me by a young Indian lad. It was at one time a robe of ceremony and falls to my ankles in long soft folds of many colors. All blending gradually like the green and purple and blue and gray of an evening in Taos.

And all of my friends are artists of one sort or another. They are all very much interested in that which they do. And in that which I do also.

I write poems now. No longer do I merely think them. I am the author of a book of Negro poems. And another of Indian poems. And they are published by my stepfather's firm, and the name of the author is called Aeon. Siempre is proud of me. People went to know me. And my poems can be Negroid yet only add greatness to me, so strange is it that a white poet can so become a part of emotions Negro. Or Indian. For I translate Indian verse and discover forgotten voodoo meanings in scarce remembered Negro songs and stories. I become interested in the anthropological discrepancies extant amidst so socially different a group. And ache to be big enough to prove my theories of equalities, mental, physical, spiritual, cultural, by saying I am a Negro. Yet can I only say in poem:

Silhouette
On the face of the moon
Am I.
A dark shadow in the light.
A silhouette am I
On the face of the moon
Lacking color
Or vivid brightness
But defined all the clearer
Because I am dark,
Black on the face of the moon.
A shadow am I
Growing in the light,
Not understood as in the day,
But more easily seen

Because
I am a shadow in the light.

But only am I poet. And Siempre paints.

Days, nights, mornings, noons, all become merely or greatly, flowing time and content. But also must I remember that this Taos interlude is limited. And that I must on my return to New York carry with me to be published the works of poets whom I have found.

Also must I carry as an excuse another group of my poems. Then, too, is there that which I do not admit even to myself. I desire to see and feel the city. So I follow my reputation and return to New York. So as to experience the joy of returning to Siempre after being in New York. And to see Shep.

*****

I am walking to meet Shep. Shep is my only friend. He will sometimes be with me when he is not writing. For he is also an author`. I have known him now forever in a close way. This is sudden knowledge. But no less true.

Shep is heartbreak. And his eyes dart quick truths to become obscured and tangled in their long lashes. Never has freedom hemmed me in as it does through his friendship. Yet is his lank length the embodiment of all I am not to trust through heritage—he is white and a Southerner. Emotion for him torrents so full through me that my glances likewise become tangled in his long lashes. To him only dare I confide my color and race through lack of color. For he also thinks naked. In beauty of the one for the one has he through not trying, proved him to me. And my love for him is greater than my love for else, for in him do I find the vessel in which to pour me and all of me that I may through his eyes discover the secret corners of me. He is my cross and religion. For never before have I been with complete- friend.

It is a pleasant thing to toss a frightened sacred thought to another and have it return sacred. Always before have I had to weave my gardens with no soothing sea nearby to lull and revive me. And, as through Beama, all love passed as through a filter, now through him do all thoughts, deeds and emotions pass.

I wonder what he would think of my Harlem episode. I walk on. Shep is taking me to a party at Serge Von Vertner's. I walk on. Is there a moon? Is that gray, shoddy arc the moon? My footsteps weep into the night. Even the moon is worn out. Broken. The streets gray. With black spots. The streets are worn. Has one a soul? Only an ache. A heavy gray ache like the moon. The buildings. Broken, blind. Many eyes worn out with watching. Only one bright window. The windows are the eyes of the buildings. And they are dark. All but one. Are one's eyes, windows of the soul in poet taste, are one's eyes dark too. Like the windows, worn out with watching. That one light window. It looks so gray. But from it comes sounds. Mournful sounds. Blues. Even the brave window is growing tired. One does weep before the lights go out.

The brave window is worn out. One's tears do give out. One's soul does grow tired. Even the wind is tired. Listless. Spent when it reaches me. Maybe the river. When one is tired, the river offers. But the river is low, sluggish, warm on its way to the sea. Has the river a soul? Is it worn out too? Tired? Tired. Oh, the soft caress of waters. Soothing.

Soothing the broken arc, the soul . . . the tired windows. The worn streets . . . the wind. It begins to rain and I walk on. To meet Shep. It rains and rains, and I walk on.

Rain. Like black opals in the hollows of obsidian bowls. A black flame would be beautiful. Wet asphalt veined with light. Like black marble. A black flame would be beautiful. A white horse passes with a proud arched neck. And in a lighted pool is one inverted. Rain. Casting white shadows of white horses. Rain filling obsidian bowls with black opals. Rain giving birth to rippling reflections and melancholy desires. Rain is a prayer. Offering black opals in obsidian bowls and white horses with proud arched necks. One upright and one inverted. Offering many hallowed beryls in converging rows. Offering me. A black flame would be beautiful. Sing a dream, sing a dream, sing a dream flame.

The shower is over. And now it is no longer raining. The moon happens again.

Refreshed and pale from its immersion in the wet black night. And I am moon color. My dark background seems merely to have emphasized my paleness. And I become frightened when I think that the moon and I are as one. Above me, before me, is the moon. I think of Siempre. Before me the moon glides in the night. Always before me. I stop and so does the moon. Above me, before me. I light a cigarette and think of Siempre. I walk on and the moon glides on before me. Above and before me. Faster, faster. And the moon also. I must catch the moon. Try and catch the moon. This has all happened before. I walk faster, faster. And the moon is always before me faster, faster. I run now. Faster. Faster and catch the moon. Running swiftly on the street, on the narrow blue. And the moon sails above me.

Before me. Like a silver coin thrown across the sea. Faster. I breathe with difficulty.

*****

I only stay a short while at the party. I come in. I greet people. I leave. But not before I meet Stuartt and Rusty and Myra. They are Negroes. Through Shep I have met Myra.

There is Rose McClendon. Who is the personification of many beauties. There are more than many beauties. There is greatness-all-the-more-great because it is so indigenous. She is with beauty replete. She is an actress, a great one. She is a Negro and one of the three greatest actresses on the American stage. She is race-proud with greater pride than can most people have without being by it consumed and is without race prejudice. She is great with genius and knowledge of that genius and is humble before her gifts and proud within them. She is the most complete person whom ever I shall know. She is great because greatness has chosen her.

And Barthe. He is a Negro. Barthe is a sculptor because he will be a sculptor. He paints and I can see that there is more than color or form to be seen. There is also vision. He is mystic and religiously catholic while catholically religious. His superstitions are from the Negro prime of him. That is good. He has shrewdness and kindness and the each uses well the other while each is at the same time individual and in itself honest. And in their computability within him become in their amalgam honesty likewise. He is a great sculptor because he will see to it that the world knows him as such and demands from him the produce of greatness in sculpture. He has chosen his path and will adhere to it. He is great be-cause he has chosen greatness.

And I meet Stuartt. Who is my brother, a son of my parents, and who seems to know it not. For we have known each other only slightly. And then in childhood. We are now adult and he has left us to be with those whom he may know. He has remained colored. And is happy, his pale skin warmed by the glow of his darker-skinned friends. He writes and paints and. loves. But mostly loves. He is young. Nineteen. And his loves lie in his eyes and challenge decency and convention and the white world. Sex is of no importance to him. Nor number. He loves women, he loves men, individually and emotionally, and submits physically to either, that they be paid for the stimuli they afford him. The stimuli without which he cannot live. And all this lies in his innocent sexual eyes and trails through his trivial, but perfect and decadent, arts. And this is my brother who knows me not. He knows me not nor shall I know him.

But I find myself likewise snared by his eyes and throat and decide to know him casually well. Perhaps through him I can glimpse that for which I long.

And I meet Myra. Myra is brown and so very all that I am not. She is Negro as I would be. She is with sex unconsciously overflowing. And we meet. She is more naive than I had remembered possible. She is the American Negro. Not the one who is as I: who am not typical nor the black who is tenement rather peasant. But she is so very average, in intelligence, and understanding, in desires and taboo. And being to her as white, I am taboo sexually, socially, even more than not being married to her am I taboo socially, sexually.

But also am I, since taboo and opposite, even more desirable. And she is all that I must possess. Through whom to arrive at rock-race-bottom at last . . . I am after all only half-high.

AND...

Myra adores me with her eyes and every gesture. I am having dinner with Myra and am still Aeon seeing Myra for the first time, when Shep called me over to meet: her at Serge's party. Am still Aeon who calls sedately on her, waiting in a precise perfect parlor, and takes her to sepia social soirees, where I am viewed by nice Negroes because, although they know I am white, they feel that soon I can be so one of them, through Myra, as to no longer warrant other than acceptance. Am still Aeon who finds himself becoming Myra's beau, and revels in the safe colour of that position. Am still Aeon who is now, vicariously, the product of Negro and Nordic who are each the product of Negro-Nordic and Nordic- Negro, who are one the product of Nordic and Nordic maybe, the other the product of Negro and Negro maybe. But only in my mind is this possible and then only because, through being beau to Myra, do I become coloured by her and her coloured surroundings.

We are having dinner in a little French restaurant downtown. Myra toys with her glass as she speaks.

"Aeon, you won't think me silly if I tell you something, will you?" I make patterns with burnt match stems and repeat, "Silly, Myra?" To which encouragement she answers, "Well, do you know, I, of course, know it is a sacrilege and I should not say it, but you do know that you look like . . . just like . . ." and she whispers, " . . . Jesus." "I suppose I shouldn't even think it but I do. And other people think so too," she adds defensively. I am silent as she looks at me. Then do I feel the Baptist Amen of child fervor proving that only through forbidden glory can my dream remain real. And I become clever. So clever that I become the cynical clever aloud that has surrounded the name of the poet, Aeon. And since that cleverness amounts to merely the saying of the obvious, to be startling, and in a voice made blank and beautiful like poetry, so that truth, cynicism, sarcasm or prophecy can be held all depending on the vision, desire or interpretation by the listener, I answer:

"I am! No, don't start, Myra. Do not think I am poking fun at you. Listen one minute." Then I take in my unbelieving hands her belief to weld my unbelievable myth into belief for her. I pose my tale in prophet prose that is all poetry because I am creating a religion and I find myself growing interested in my own myth and the necessity of correlating dates and names of interest in their logical and sound juxtaposition. And my explanation that I am Jesus is merely as I say in these words:

"You see, Myra, as Jesus, it was the desire of God, my Father, that I by my deaths expiate the sins of the world. But God is a Just God and conceived that I must sin, that the sins of the world be justly on my shoulders. And so that I might live forever, and living be eternally dying. The story of my first sin is history. Why, Myra, do you think God let me die? So that I might sit on his right hand and be idle? Does that seem like the wisdom of a god? You know how soon a lesson told is forgotten. So God had me sin, and die, that I might be born again from the womb of the woman with whom I sinned. On the night when I felt my breath and blood failing me on the cross, when my eyes were becoming clouded as night, with dying, I saw light, and did not recognize it, felt hands be tender and did not know them. For to me was even it a great thing. A great thing that the hands that had caressed me on that cross, between thieves, should give sensations that were the loving hands of a mother with her just-born babe. For even as you might dream it is a flower brushing your lips, and waken to find it is in reality a kiss of love, so was my passage from the dream of dying to the reality of rebirth. And I grew. And life was. And always was I afraid that at sometime would I love a woman and in procreation die again.

"Always I knew that I could not suffer alone. And that is the way in which I atone for the sins of the world. As example, my first death, the death of Jesus, allowed me to be reborn as Clemons Romaus, first bishop of Rome, then as the kindly church-father of Palestine, Justin Martyr; and subsequently as Father Flavius Clemens; as Arta-xerxes, the Persian who founded the Sassanian dynasty. And so on through Emperor Diocletian Jovius, Bishop Cyril of Alexandria, Pope Leo the, First, called the Great; Dionysius Exigue Abbot of Rome; Khusrau, a Sassanide king of Persia; Abu-Hafsah-ibn- al-Khattab; Omar the First, who was captor of Jerusalem. You see, Myra, I could go right on through, year for year, through the centuries, and name them each, but instead, now that you know, it suffices to mention such names as: Richard Coeur de Lion, Georg van Peuerbach, the Italian painter Francesco Primaticcio, Frantsek Palacky, Carlo Passaglia, theologian, and...well...

"And here I am . . ." and I can see that Myra is impressed nearly to belief through the logic of my cleverspun fantasy.

And I realize that my myth has penetrated beneath her modernity and intelligence to touch the Negro prime of her. I have too cleverly with logic offered names to which she has educationally furnished dates which but corroborate the possibility of the impossible for her. And her love for me causes belief and fear of the truth she now knows is true. My myth has swept me nearer her so that now she is inaccessible because of love for me. For she believes that I might die should she be with child for me—and believes that she would be with child for me did we love. For what safeguard could she use that would not be blasphemous? That would not be Christ-killing. All this I sense from her refusals and kisses. And so desire her more and with yet greater desire. For this would in truth be plumbing rock-race bottom and love depths I've never known.

*****

Once I take her to a Harlem theatre and we see the show as through love for each other. A set of dancers appears. They are called "DARKTOWN'S DAPPER DANCERS" and are Rio, Rhythm and Honey. Rhythm is my youngest brother, whom also I know not. Who also is not with us as family. I know this youngest brother of mine before even I recognize his smile, which he has retained from even greater youth. I ask Myra, to whom everyone in Harlem is known, to introduce me. And when I meet my brother and hold his hand I feel the warmth of his smile as, impersonally he says, "Pleased to meetcha—see you, Myra." And he smiles in a way to me.

And this encounter with my youngest brother, whom I think likewise and in the same way knows that I am his brother, leaves me sad in an objective way and desiring assurance of being through Myra even more. For I have no family but mother—and there is of it nothing save only recognition of love the one for the other. Manifestations of clan are as non-existent as is the call of clan so psychically felt.

*****

A lamblike March. A soothing spring Sunday. Seventh Avenue. Forms flowing along on a soothing spring Sunday. Down Seventh Avenue. In jazz rhythms. An undulating hodge-podge of colour and form. Forms and colours on a soothing spring Sunday and a lamblike March oozing with warmth and rhythm on Seventh Avenue. There is an urgence in the air. An urgence akin to madness. Motivating laughter. Laughing forms tinted with colour jumbled with jazz rhythm. Seeking seering salvation on Seventh Avenue. The devil has been loosed. Loosed from his pit in hell. To shed the chains of eternity to stroll down Seventh Avenue on a soothing spring Sunday. Strolling like a chameleon. Dancing a Charleston. God is good. The devil has been loosed. Praise God. Praise the saints. The devil is loose. Loose—and forms flow down Seventh Avenue, a hodge-podge of colour and futility. Harlem! God is good. But the angels know God and Lucifer defied Him before man was man. Or the earth the earth or the sun a sun. God. A dissembled body bloated with cosmic urge. God is mad. His head is filled with images and shadows and tongues of flame. Buddha was God. Yellow and complacent like an acid-scarred beetle in a sunflower feud. Mohammed was God. With a will like waves tortured and spewed by tremulous tides. Jove was God. A slug of finite thunder torn from infinite mountain tops. Mumbo-Jumbo was God. With a kink in his hair and tattoo on his cheek.

And Brahma, and Isis and Krishna and Thor. Fading faggots in eternities fire shedding light to multitudes of morons.

White Christ.

Christ was a man. With the power to procreate. Who was crucified on the cross at Calvary. While Jove roared through the clouds— Buddha uprooted transient souls— Krishna smiled—Mumbo-Jumbo added a plume to his headdress—Brahma brooded and the Holy Ghost merged with the devil in hell. Christ was God. I am God. Must fume like a peacock over a brilliant tailfeather spawned in the night while the senses slept.

Creation has begun and I have proven the function of man. And beside breathes gently with sweet, opened mouth, the girl who has known for me Harlem.: She is pale red- black, and is beauty. It is day and I see that the creases in my mental folds sag as salaciously as do those of the landlady's face, who announces through a crack in the closed door that breakfast is ready.

And as I lie in sun and feel the love of Myra besides me, I am drowned in smug well- being which yet is cosmic content. Which I shatter with externals when Myra looks at me heavy with love and forgetful of fear. For I whisper cleverly—crucified—and the love and fear and pain in her face are so great a poem that I am ashamed. For

I had only half believed. I had not thought it possible for one to be so complete in belief of love and belief as she—and I console her as best I can—which is only to kiss her and love her. But her pain I cannot touch—for it is out of her love and she is whole—and I—I am half-high.

And always now there is for me Myra in New York to give me race through love for me. And Siempre in Taos to give me even love through also loving and being loved by me.

I return to Taos. But in reality to Siempre. And Myra becomes a poem for me to write by day. A feeling for me to flounder through as I closely love and caress Siempre. The warmth of the colour of Myra punctuates my work, even as through remembrance of it am I more expert and real to Siempre. Through the dream which screams out contacts, Siempre finds my soul. And this depth she recognizes as aroused for her, though she cannot know through whom. Nor how nebulous is this tangible emotion.

I cannot clearly see this thing for myself. How, through finding race bottom in all ways, of sex, of mind, emotion, and environment through Myra, it makes greater my love for Siempre who is as white. Nor will I admit my white bloods, since with the reactions of my black am I replete. But I am stirred vaguely even through my pleasure and content.

Stirred to problems I must solve. About me.

As I think of the possible outcome of having known Myra, I become also aware of her belief in my myth. And recognize the possible cruelty of me. Only can I feel displeasure because I am no more contrite. For I know, that if Myra should have child, her belief through belief itself and magnified by fearful love for me, would convince her she had murdered me. And if I do not die, and through her child-birth prove my truth, I destroy likewise in myself a symbol. A symbol which I have always mis-sought:

That Siempre remarks also that I look like Jesus, stirs more violently the fragments I disbelieve with my mind, even as I recognize and admit then with emotions. And every day, intellect and emotions become more irreconciliable. I grow irritable and feverish. I decide to see Shep. He alone through being alone can justify me to myself.

So I come again, after seven months, to New York.

*****

I am going to meet Shep in his rooms. And as I mount in the lift I wonder at the strong friendship that is grown up between us. To him only do I turn. And also do I think of my first meeting with him and of being so impressed with the hidden things piercing with brightness his meager exterior. And now I have much to tell him. There is my not-love for Myra. With psychological parabolas to define. And poetic success. With retrousse emotions parqueted in oblique patterns of perception.

I knock at his door and am bid enter. Shep is replete in chamois knickers, high mahogany sheen boots and cream flannelled shirt. We drink. We talk. And he is unravelling my perplexed flounderings. I tell him I see no end or reason to myself and life. Which statement he refutes. I am sitting near the window fourteen stories high above Tenth Street.

And he refutes me, throwing open wide the window to the floor, saying, "There is reason though, for you to find, because is not the view from here pleasant. There is reason enough if you sit fourteen stories high and talk, or you would instead walk and keep walking out on the air so—."

And Shep has walked out of the window to which I rush to see him climb in grotesque patterns too rapidly down through the air. And melt into a slight unimportant heap as he strikes the pavement. A woman who has been walking toward the now important spot faints. An automobile shrills to a standstill and empties a man sick with the vision of Shep in falling. And there is a crowd as excited as I should be, who now descend to take calm charge of the body. He had landed on his feet and his mahogany sheen boots are split to the knee. I give all particulars to all necessary persons and realize that now I have no friend.

In the heads of mummies buried deep under many stone blocks brought for miles through heat and sands by thousands of slaves working many years, bleeding, sweating under the sting of lashes, perspiration salting their wounds and speeding their lagging tired muscles, and causing waking dreams of rest to blind with pleasure their stinging eyes is a miracle so called. Under tons of rocks called pyramids, after one delves into carved stone sarcophagi, to find the gilded wooden caskets within. And comes at last to the ossified remains of some king or queen or potentate, wrapped many times in worn and spiced linen, there is thought. Thought is a fly. Generations of communing with the dead. Centuries of solitude have given it short space in which to meditate. Segregation is with it as it has been with me for there is nothing to all these fine wrappings. Nor is there pomp left nor truth of the belief even of that ideal in which life roots. Ideal that buzzes around with the meaningless hum of a fly. In the crypt and close to the emptiness of all that was power and living and glory and hope there is this fly. And in the shell of me there is also Sarcophagae Metabunda.

If I would die it should be a city death and earth-bound. Not epic—but casual as death is casual. An added incident of traffic occurrence. A slight distortion of life. A minute distortion of habit— come slow and unaware or, aware and yet more slow. Like understanding. I have no friend. Nor am I complete in the loves I have. I have built the I I am to Myra and it is not I even while it is more truly I. I have grown the I I am to Siempre even while taking from me the life I would have had had I not breathed it through love to her. I have pulsed the songs I sing and they are merely the echo-come-sadly-distorted of the peoples from whom they spring. I am the wraith of their emotions and thoughts and wisdoms. I do not exist. They are whole. I am only half-high.

And as I walk through the streets of New York I know myself. I love Siempre. I love Beam. I love Myra. I love Shep. I love the thing of myself I now know. My ornamented emotions so woven fast with these—and with swift-moving vehicles—slow-moving love—

hesitant knowledge. And I know that which I must do—So—as I am about to cross Forty- Second Street at Broadway, I decide. And there is a moment's fear—a high exhilarating excitement before—

I step quickly from the curb. And there is a great flame in a second of pain as blackness descends tinseled with hysterical voices.

And now—in this stolen moment—as I do that which is forbidden me—and use strength they do not know I have, to write—

I love this thing of myself I know as I lie in a neat white room like a gift in a wedding box—and on the third day rose again—and ascended into—is there such phenomena as time?

I lie, beating my life into a doctor's ears through a stethoscope. Beating my life out in this hospital room with this one thing I know. That I know nothing, not even this one thing I know—fluttering blindly around and around me like—a moth—gray —

—gray—

Aeon

City Hospital
July 1926